1 2 3

PLAY WITH ME

Karen Gundersheimer

HARPER & ROW, PUBLISHERS

For my sister and brother

1 2 3 Play With Me
Copyright © 1984 by Karen Gundersheimer
Printed in the U.S.A. All rights reserved.
1   2   3   4   5   6   7   8   9   10
First Edition

Library of Congress Cataloging in Publication Data
Gundersheimer, Karen.
  1 2 3 play with me.

  Summary: With sister Minna's help, Memo the mouse
counts up all his toys, backwards and forwards.
  [1. Mice—Fiction.   2. Counting]   I. Title.
II. Title: One two three play with me.
PZ7.G96Aad 1984   [E]   84-47628
ISBN 0-06-022176-3
ISBN 0-06-022177-1 (lib. bdg.)

I'm Minna.
Memo is my little brother.
He is smart. *Very* smart.
He knows how to count.
And I taught him.
Just like this.

ONE

ONE birthday hat

TWO

TWO fuzzy puppets

THREE

THREE rag dolls

FOUR

FOUR rubber balls

FIVE

FIVE wooden beads

SIX

SIX toy trucks

SEVEN

SEVEN farm animals

EIGHT

EIGHT train cars

NINE

NINE building blocks

TEN

TEN teeny people

Memo is a messy mouse.
But smart. *Very* smart.
He even knows how to count backwards.

And how to clean up.
Because I taught him.
Just like this.

10

9

8

7

6

5

4

3

2

1

Memo is happy. *Very* happy.
He cleaned up all his toys.
Then Mama calls,
"Who wants milk and cookies?"

Can you count how many we ate?